This edition is published
and distributed exclusively by
Discovery Toys, Inc., Martinez, CA

First published in 1989 by
Walker Books, Ltd., London

©1989 Julie Lacome

Printed and bound in Hong Kong by
Sheck Wah Tong Printing Press Ltd.

ISBN 0-939979-32-2

*The Discovery Toys Book of*

# NURSERY RHYMES

## Julie Lacome

DISCOVERY TOYS, INC.

Sing a song of sixpence,
    A pocket full of rye,
Four and twenty blackbirds,
    Baked in a pie.

When the pie was opened,
    The birds began to sing;
Wasn't that a dainty dish
    To set before the king?

The king was in his counting-house,
    Counting out his money;
The queen was in the parlor,
    Eating bread and honey.

The maid was in the garden,
    Hanging out the clothes,
When down came a blackbird
    And pecked off her nose.

Here we go round the mulberry bush,
The mulberry bush, the mulberry bush,
Here we go round the mulberry bush,
So early in the morning.

This is the way we wash our hands,
Wash our hands, wash our hands,
This is the way we wash our hands,
So early in the morning.

This is the way we brush our teeth,
Brush our teeth, brush our teeth,
This is the way we brush our teeth,
So early in the morning.

This is the way we comb our hair,
Comb our hair, comb our hair,
This is the way we comb our hair,
So early in the morning.

Jack and Jill went up the hill,
    To fetch a pail of water;
Jack fell down and broke his crown,
    And Jill came tumbling after.

Up he got and home did trot,
As fast as he could caper;
And went to bed to mend his head
With vinegar and brown paper.

Little Boy Blue,
    Come blow your horn,
The sheep's in the meadow,
    The cow's in the corn.

Where is the boy
    Who looks after the sheep?
He's under a haystack
    Fast asleep.
Will you wake him?
    No, not I,
For if I do,
    He's sure to cry.

Hickory, dickory, dock,
The mouse ran up the clock.
The clock struck one,
The mouse ran down;
Hickory, dickory, dock.

See, saw, Margery Daw,
Johnny shall have a new master;
He shall have but a penny a day,
Because he can't work any faster.

Humpty Dumpty
Sat on a wall,
Humpty Dumpty
Had a great fall.

All the king's horses
And all the king's men
Couldn't put Humpty
Together again.

Yankee Doodle came to town,
   Riding on a pony;
He stuck a feather in his cap
   And called it macaroni.

Yankee Doodle keep it up,
   Yankee Doodle dandy;
Mind the music and the step,
   And with the girls be handy.

Baa baa black sheep, have you any wool?
    Yes sir, yes sir, three bags full:
One for the master and one for the dame,
    And one for the little boy who lives down the lane.

Hey diddle, diddle, the cat and the fiddle,
The cow jumped over the moon.
   The little dog laughed to see such sport,
And the dish ran away with the spoon.

Little Bo-Peep has lost her sheep,
    And doesn't know where to find them;
Leave them alone and they'll come home,
    Wagging their tails behind them.

Little Bo-Peep fell fast asleep,
    And dreamt she heard them bleating;
But when she awoke, she found it a joke,
    For they were still a-fleeting.

Then up she took her little crook,
    Determined for to find them;
She found them indeed, but it made her heart bleed,
    For they'd left all their tails behind them.

    It happened one day as Bo-Peep did stray
        Into a meadow hard by;
    There she spied their tails side by side,
        All hung on a tree to dry.

    She heaved a sigh and wiped her eye,
        Then went o'er hill and dale,
    And tried what she could, as a shepherdess should,
        To tack to each sheep its tail.

Rock-a-bye baby, on the tree top,
When the wind blows the cradle will rock;
When the bough breaks the cradle will fall,
Down will come baby, cradle, and all.

Twinkle, twinkle, little star,
How I wonder what you are!
Up above the world so high,
Like a diamond in the sky.
Twinkle, twinkle, little star,
How I wonder what you are!